EVERYTHING IS
MAMA

To Winnie, Franny, and Nancy. You are my everything.

A FEIWEL AND FRIENDS BOOK
An imprint of Macmillan Publishing Group, LLC
120 Broadway, New York, NY 10271

Our books may be purchased for promotional, educational, or business use. Please contact your local bookseller or the Macmillan Corporate and Premium Sales Department at (800) 221-7945 ext. 5442 or by email at MacmillanSpecialMarkets@macmillan.com.

Library of Congress Control Number: 2017940441

Book design by Rich Deas and Miguel Ordóñez

Feiwel and Friends logo designed by Filomena Tuosto

First edition, 2017

This special edition was printed for Kohl's, Inc. (for distribution on behalf of Kohl's Cares, LLC,
its wholly owned subsidiary) by Feiwel and Friends, an imprint of Macmillan Publishing Group, LLC.

ISBN 978-1-250-12584-2 (hardcover)

ISBN 978-1-250-89842-5 (Kohl's Exclusive)

Kohl's, Inc.
Style: 98425
Factory Number: 123386
Production Date: 12/2022

1 3 5 7 9 10 8 6 4 2

mackids.com

Ages 3 and up

EVERYTHING IS
MAMA
JIMMY FALLON

ILLUSTRATED BY MIGUEL ORDÓÑEZ

FEIWEL AND FRIENDS
NEW YORK

Everything is Mama
according to you.

But there are **other** fun words
you'll want to know, too.

HAT

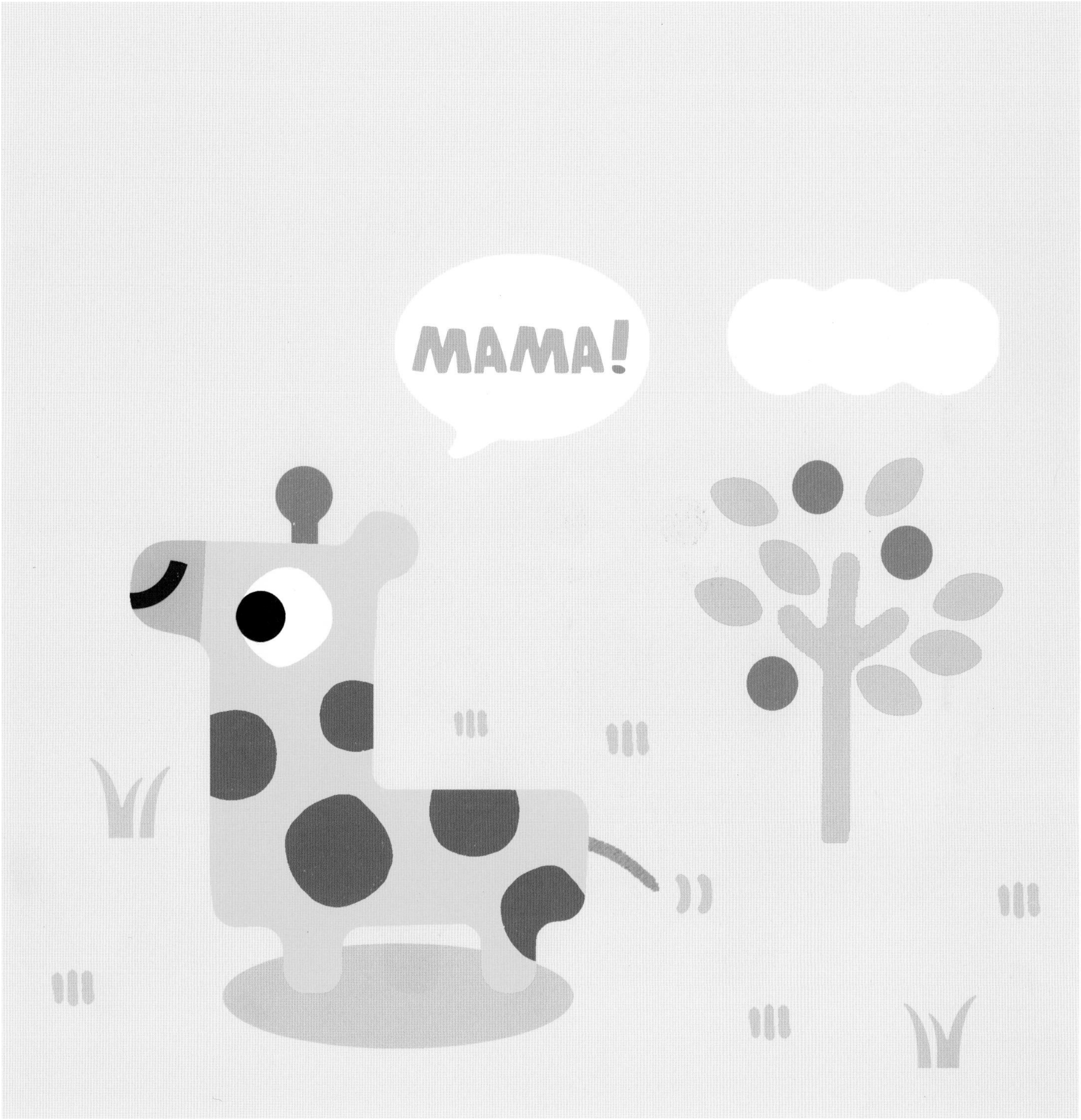
MAMA!

Everything is Mama
according to you.

But one day you'll see,
Mama's EVERYTHING is YOU.